AFTER THE SILENCE

PAUL JONES

After
The
Silence

ISBN 9798726130880

Contents

Characters

Danny, a late 20-something year old gay lad. He has model good looks and appears confident. But looks can be deceiving.

Jo, a nurse, originally from Ireland, now living in London. She is in her late 20s, is pretty, naturally pretty, and isn't wearing a lot of make-up.

Margaret, is 'mumsy'. A lovely, cuddly, tactile mum in her 50s or 60s. She is a northern lady and speaks with a Yorkshire or Lancashire lilt.

Sarah, late 20s. Blond, beautiful, an English Rose. She is Danny's best friend, the love of Jo's life and Margaret's daughter. Sarah is also dead.

Music

Songs are played at the start of each monologue. These can start before the lights go up allowing for the minimal items of set to be arranged on stage. The music continues as the lights go up and our characters enter.

After the Silence - Part I: *Danny*

Lights out as the stage is set. "Scared of the Dark" by Steps is playing.

Lights up.

ENTER Danny. Danny is a late 20 something year old lad, in ripped jeans, trainers, tight t-shirt and hoody. He has earbuds in and is listening to his Spotify playlist. He has model good looks and appears confident. But looks can be deceiving.

Danny sits on a bench, in a secluded park. It is early evening, sometime in the spring. Danny nods his head to the music. He smiles, he is enjoying the moment.

The music stops abruptly.

He stops, looks straight ahead and takes a deep breath in. The smile has gone, he looks concerned, even anxious.

Danny: It was this song. They played this song. I remember it vividly. I was in the club. The music was pumping; the bass was going right through my body. I was living my best life.

Danny removes the earbuds and tucks them into his hoody pocket.

Danny: It was a Friday night. I fuckin' love Friday nights. I'd met Sarah after work, we'd got the tube to Leicester Square and then walked up to her favourite bar. Her girlfriend was working late, so it was just the two of us. Me and Sarah. Sarah and me. Besties since ... forever! We went to this bar for a drink. There was a huge neon arse in the window and an endless happy hour. A couple of shots and a cocktail or two for me, and Jo, that's Sarah's girlfriend, WhatsApped her. She's a nurse; Jo. A&E at St. Thomas' - she was always working late, especially at the weekends.

Danny shifts on the bench and then looks ahead; he smiles.

Danny: Sarah was so pissed off; like she was sooooo cross. *Danny imitates Sarah's voice and screws his face up.* "She's not coming, gotta work til 12 and then going to bed. It's fuckin' Friday and she's not coming." *Danny returns to himself, smiling.* I looked at her; I smiled at her. Everyone falls for a Danny-boy smile. 'Let's get wrecked' I told her.

Danny puts his hands on his knees, and then sits back. He smiles to himself and then looks ahead, re-engaging us.

Danny: Sooooo we ended up in this club. Rainbowz. With a Z. I got us a couple of vodka cokes and dragged Sarah onto the dance floor. I downed mine, she didn't touch hers. She was being a right moody bitch but this was Friday night and I was in the mood to party. "Snap out of it", I told her. "We can have a laugh. We are gonna get pissed and dance the night away. Forget Jo. You can be pissed off with her when you get in, kip on the couch to show her how shitty you feel and then have THE best make up sex in the morning".

Danny pauses and smiles a big, wide smile.

Danny: After a few cheesy 90s pop songs and some Lady Gaga, Sarah was having a laugh and finally letting her hair down. We had a few more vodka cokes - well I did, some shots that looked and tasted like Listerine and a jägerbomb or two. Sarah kept getting water and orange juice, said she needed a clear head to deal with Jo! Whatever! Sooooo I kept smiling at this cute-as-fuck lad behind Sarah. He'd taken his top off and was dancing on his own across the other side of the dancefloor. I kept giving him my cheeky Dannyboy smile but it wasn't working. He was oblivious. Sarah noticed and put her arms around me; then she shouted into my ear. *Danny imitates Sarah again.* "He's off his tits babe. He's probably on something".

Danny looks down at the ground and shifts his feet. He clasps his hand, lets go and looks ahead. The smile fades, he refocuses and a small glimmer of a smile crosses his mouth.

Danny: Then this song came on. Steps - 'Scared of the Dark'. Sarah and I went wild. We loved this song. We'd always been massive Steps fans as kids. We were like soooo young when they were big. We'd dress up and I'd always want to be Claire, but Sarah was Claire and I was H. I was secretly pleased; even as a kid I thought he was cute. So we were well chuffed when they came back and 'Scared of the Dark' became our anthem.

Danny stops. He shifts awkwardly and then looks forward, troubled, anxious, hurt.

Danny: We were dancing, loving it. It was such a buzz, such a good night. It all happened so fast and yet time seemed to slow right down and even stopped. One minute Steps euphoria, the next ... chaos.

Danny pauses.

Danny: This bloke came from nowhere, he pushed Sarah and punched me in the face. He started shouting something, which I couldn't hear. I'd stumbled backwards and lost my balance. The dancefloor lights switched from red to green to yellow. My ears were ringing and my face was throbbing with pain.

And then, as I steadied myself and stood up, I saw the disco lights switch back to red and the anger on this bloke's face was framed in a crimson glow. That's when I first saw it. A glint of metal, a flash of light as the colours changed. A blade.

Danny takes a longer pause.

Danny: The doormen were everywhere, on top of this guy dragging him away. The music stopped and the people around us were screaming, scattering away from the dancefloor. Sheer panic. I remember falling to my knees and looking at my hands. The club lights flickered on and then I saw the blood on my hands. Someone ran over with a first aid kit, they were grabbing at bandages, pads, dressings. Shock. I think I was in shock.

Danny looks at his hands and back up again.

Danny: Blood everywhere, and then I knew. It wasn't my blood. And in that split second, the ringing in my ears stopped. The throbbing in my jaw ceased. There was total ... and utter... silence. The silence was only a split second in my mind, but the silence lasted an eternity.

Danny swallows, his eyes welling up.

Danny: I went in the ambulance with her. The paramedics told me that she'd been stabbed in the neck. She'd got stabbed trying to save me.

Tears roll down Danny's cheeks.

Danny: I remember talking to her, I remember holding her, willing her to be alright. Her blood on my hands, her life in my hands. The music stopped and in my head a ringing and then silence.

Danny wipes the tears.

Danny: When we got to the hospital, they stopped me going with her. I had to wait as they took her away. That silence came back and it was all around me. The bustling waiting area, full of drunks and druggies, was so busy but my head was filled with silence. Until a noise pierced the silence, an everlasting shrillness, a scream. Jo!

Danny takes a breath, wipes his tears.

Danny: I knew when I heard Jo scream that the silence was over. But I knew for Sarah the silence was just beginning. And for Sarah, the silence was now eternal.

Lights fade.

After the Silence - Part II: *Jo*

Lights out as "Bad Romance" by Lady Gaga is playing.

Lights up.

ENTER Jo. Jo is a nurse, originally from Ireland, now living in London. She is in her late 20s, in blue NHS scrubs, with an NHS lanyard around her neck, three different coloured biros in her scrubs' top pocket and an NHS LGBT+ rainbow badge on her tunic. She is wearing a zipped-up navy hoody over her scrubs and has earbuds in. Jo is pretty, naturally pretty, and isn't wearing a lot of make-up.

Jo walks on and stops.

The music stops as Jo removes her earbuds.

Jo: It was this song. I played this song. I remember it vividly. I was on the tube going home after a looooong shift and a group of girls got on at Embankment. They were all dressed up with somewhere to go, and I just wanted my PJs and something hot and milky.

I plugged myself in, not to be antisocial, but when you've had a day of ingrowing toenails, hypochondriacs and Junior Doctors I just needed to switch off. First song that came on was Lady Gaga - “Bad Romance”. ‘Isn’t that just the story of my life?’ I thought, ‘Bad romance, followed by worse romance, followed by... well NO romance’. I turned the volume up and just let the music drown out the girls - I guessed they’d all get out at Leicester Square and then I could finish my journey home in peace.

Jo wraps the earbuds around her phone and puts her phone in her hoody pocket.

Jo: It didn’t last; the peace. Literally seconds out of the station; we’d not even reached Charing Cross; and this drunken girl, landed in the seat next to me. *Jo pauses.* I don’t know which came first - the annoyance or the overwhelming fluttering of butterflies at the sight of her smile. *Jo scowls.* It was definitely the annoyance... *Jo melts into a smile.* ... but wow, this girl was hot. I mean like really hot. Like some kind of... fallen angel, well landed angel. 'Cos there she was, landed next to me. Smiling, and then giggling. I remember her speaking, but I was still listening to my music, and couldn't hear a word she was saying. I didn't need to; those butterflies were telling me everything I needed to hear. "Sarah" she said. "I'm Sarah."

Jo unzips her hoody and shuffles awkwardly, shyly, hands in her pockets.

Jo: I don't know how it does it; The Universe I mean. Two random lesbians in the right place, at the right time, on the right tube, and that moment of pure electricity. It was like some chemical reaction and suddenly all the atoms were aligned, or fizzing, or just saying in the most random way - "Jo, this is the girl for you!".

Jo takes her hands out of her pockets and regains her self-confidence.

Jo: Three years next month. Three years since we moved in together and it was the happiest day of my life. It's amazing how you spend days on end longing for something, wishing you had something, and then when you find it those days of emptiness just disappear. Life was great. Me and Sarah, Sarah and me; I knew she was forever. My eternity, well... our eternity. You see when I started dating Sarah, I didn't just get the girl of my dreams, I also got her somewhat irritating, but equally charming GBF - and pseudo brother - Danny.

Jo looks directly forward, adopting a serious tone.

Jo: Have you ever tried dating somebody when date night becomes a '*menage a trois*', and I don't mean in a good way? Date nights with Sarah, invariably became date nights with Sarah and Danny... it was like dating Ant and Dec. There were three of us in this relationship, only the third wheel did nothing for me...or Sarah.

Jo relaxes again, smiling.

Jo: I got used to it, to be honest, Sarah and Danny and me. To be fair, we'd have a laugh on our legendary nights out in

Soho. We'd go out, get pissed, down several more shots than our livers could handle and then Danny would cop off with some handsome bloke and Sarah and I would console him in the Uber on the way home when he realised 'Mr Fit' wasn't forever. It became our thing, and I enjoyed it secretly; we all did. We were living the dream.

Jo shifts her weight and looks uneasy; something is wrong.

Jo: Until this one Friday night; a few weeks ago. I was going to meet them in Soho, some bar with a huge neon arse in the window. I'd change out of my scrubs, get the tube to Leicester Square and be there in time for their fourth, or fifth cocktail. Only, it didn't work like that - we got busy, really busy and the 2iC asked me to stay late; shift some of the drunks out of the cubicles and on their merry way. Me, being a dedicated, caring health professional agreed and I WhatsApped Sarah to wish her a good night and told her I'd see her in the morning. I knew, I knew she'd be pissed off but after a few hours of her kipping on the sofa...and snoring... she'd forgive me and we'd have the best sex ever, and maybe a bacon sandwich in bed for brunch!

Jo smiles.

Jo: So I put my phone in my locker and went back to work, looking forward to the make-up sex and bacon roll and ketchup combo!

Jo pulls her hoody round her and looks anxious.

Jo: It was somewhere after eleven, maybe closer to twelve. You kind of lose track in St. Thomas' A&E on a Friday night. We got a trauma call through, ambulance on the way in with a young, female stabbing victim. *Jo switches to professional mode*. Those minutes, before the ambulance arrives, are like preparing for battle. Getting ready for the front line. Gloves on, apron on, trolleys ready, equipment ready. You're on standby, on alert, for whatever comes through those doors; for *whoever* comes through those doors. You're prepared for anything, you have to be; you're about to fight fuckin' hard to save someone's life.

Jo wells up, a tear in the corner of her eye. She wipes it away.

Jo: Prepared. We were all prepared. And then the doors opened and the paramedics came in. I saw the trolley. The patient. Her hair. The blood. The blood was everywhere; there was so much blood.

Jo pauses, regains her composure slightly.

Jo: It is so noisy in a busy trauma room when the paramedics are handing over a patient. They're telling you the history, giving you information; the doctors are calling out instructions, telling you what they need. It happens so fast, it happens automatically, your adrenaline rushes and it's fight or flight, only you are not fighting for yourself, you're fighting for them. Helpless and lifeless, they need you. And the noise, the noise is just incredible; chaotic, but ordered. *Jo pauses.* Except that day.

Jo stops, takes a deep breath and the tears well up again.

Jo: When I saw her hair, the blood had stained her beautiful hair, I knew before the paramedic said her name. It was Sarah. Realisation... then silence... fear, adrenaline, fear, anger, fear, silence. Then I screamed. A few moments maybe, but for me eternity.

Lights fade.

<u>After the Silence - Part III: *Margaret*</u>

Lights out whilst the stage is set. "Abide with Me", the hymn, by The Oxford Trinity Choir is playing.

Lights up.

ENTER Margaret. Margaret is 'mumsy'. A lovely, cuddly, tactile mum in her 50s or 60s. Margaret is wearing a blouse, cardigan and a pair of her old gardening trousers. She has a pair of gardening gloves on. She is a northern lady and speaks with a Yorkshire or Lancashire lilt.

A bistro set is centre stage, two chairs and a round table. Margaret walks on; there is a plant on the table, which she attends to, pruning it with a pair of secateurs. She stops, removes her gloves, lays them down on the table and sits in one of the chairs.

The music fades.

Margaret: It were this song. They sang this song at my Grandad's funeral. I remember it vividly, as if it were yesterday. I can remember most things as if they were yesterday. *Slight, reflective pause.* Except perhaps yesterday, ironically.

Margaret chuckles to herself and then smiles fondly.

Margaret: (singing) Abide with me, fast falls the eventide, the darkness deepens, Lord with me abide. *A brief pause.* When you're singing that in church, I don't know but it feels a bit gloomy. I suppose it would, it's funereal isn't it. I suppose it's meant to be gloomy.

Margaret unbuttons her cardigan and places it over the table. She looks over to

her right.

Margaret: Do you know I remember when they moved in next door. The new family. Our Sarah must have been about five or six, and she came racing into the garden to tell me there was a new boy next door, and he had a BMX. She was that excited, that's the thing with 'er being an only child - with Old Mrs Lucas the other side and only a handful of kids down the street, she had no-one to play with… 'cept at school. She wanted someone in the street. Someone she could knock for, someone she could queue up at the ice-cream van with, someone to go over the rec' with. And 'ere 'e was.

Margaret sits back in the chair, smiling, reminiscing.

Margaret: He was a nice lad, the lad next door. Danny Hutchinson. Even when he was a youngster, I knew he was ... you know, the other way inclined. My old mum would have called him queer, but you can't say that anymore. Well, you couldn't, not for a long time. Turns out nowadays you can. Back in fashion, I s'pose, bit like mini skirts. Anyway, he was gay Danny, but that was fine with me and Malcolm... at least we didn't have to worry about him stopping over and getting up to no good with our Sarah.

Margaret chuckles again.

Margaret: They were inseparable, all through primary school, all through secondary school. Even went off to the same uni. together. You couldn't part them. Malcolm and I thought they could've got married and been happy, except

Danny was gay... and so was our Sarah we found out.

Margaret pauses, a little more serious.

Margaret: The night she told us; well I don't mind admitting that we were a little taken aback. I mean we accepted Danny being gay, as if 'e were our own, but she was our own and it's harder when it's your own. Malcolm was desperate for grandkiddies; we both were, but Sarah coming out - well, we didn't reckon grandkiddies were ever going to come to fruition. Until Jo that was.

Another smile.

Margaret: When she brought Jo here for her first Sunday roast it was like... it was like everything fell into place. It all made sense. She was happy. They both were. I could see it. The love in their eyes, the way they looked at each other, the way they smiled. That day was the day that it all made sense, for me anyhow. I remember thinking, before Jo, that I'd lost our Sarah - that her being a lesbian was putting a rift between us. Now I know that's wrong, but she was my daughter - and I always thought she'd have a husband - and kiddies. But with Jo it suddenly dawned on me. I'd not lost a daughter at all, I'd gained another one.

Margaret pauses and a tear wells up in the corner of her eye. She looks sombre.

Margaret: When there was that knock at the door we knew it were bad news. No-one knocks in the early hours for anything good. The policewoman told us she'd been stabbed, "fatally wounded" she said. We just couldn't take it in. Malcolm sobbed, she'd always been a daddy's girl. I just felt numb, and cold... ever so cold. Do you know, the first thought that went through my head was how much I'd lost. Not just our Sarah, not just the here and now, but the future. I wouldn't see her marry Jo, like they were planning. We wouldn't hear the laughter of grandchildren in the garden. There'd be no more Sunday roasts and no more Sarah, Jo and Danny photos on facebook. In one cruel moment, one stupid, violent moment, that's all been taken away from me... and Malcolm. And Jo.

Margaret pauses.

Margaret: I sat there, hearing the policewoman's kind, sympathetic words, but the words were just words. I was lost in my thoughts. The here and now, this awful, awful night, the future ... and the past. It struck me how much I'd lost in our past. I hate to admit it but I'd pushed her away for years after she came out; I held her at arm's length, but all that seems so stupid now. Those wasted years grieving for absolutely no reason, and yet now, in this silent moment, I've lost her for good.

Lights fade.

<u>After the Silence - Part IV: *Danny*</u>

Lights out whilst the stage is set. "Everybody Hurts" by REM is playing.

Lights up.

ENTER Danny. Danny is a late 20 something year old lad, in grey, cotton tracksuit bottoms, trainers and a baggy jumper. He has model good looks, but his confidence is hiding beneath a veil of grief.

Danny walks on and sits on a plastic, waiting room chair. One of a row of five plastic waiting room chairs. There is a coffee table to the side with well-thumbed women's magazines and a pot plant, probably artificial, that has seen better days.

Danny looks tired, solemn, a broken man.

The music fades out.

Danny: It was this song. This song on the radio. On the... on the day of her funeral. I remember it vividly. It was like it was playing just for us, for her family, her friends, for Jo. "Everybody Hurts" - we were all hurting, all in pain.

Danny pauses.

Danny: I couldn't look at Margaret or Malcolm, her parents, couldn't look them in the eye. They told me it wasn't my fault, but I knew what they were thinking - if only she hadn't been with me in the club that night, she'd still be here. She'd still be alive. They'd still have their beautiful daughter.

And Jo, I will never forget her scream in the hospital that night. It pierced the silence and shattered my heart, and now it lives on, every day, every day in my head. *Danny starts to get agitated and tenses up.* It just goes round and round tormenting me, accusing me, blaming me. It just does not relent... ever. It just won't leave me alone.

Another pause, he calms a little, but the tears are welling up.

Danny: Of course, she never blamed me either. She was more worried about me losing Sarah, my best friend. In those long, empty days before her funeral, when she should have been consumed with grief about the love of her life, she was worried about me. But she didn't stop; she became practical - she was on the phone to Margaret planning the funeral, on the phone to me checking I was ok. Organising flowers and hymns and sandwiches with Sarah's mum. She was so fucking strong, and there was me - lying in bed 'til lunchtime crying like a baby, playing that night over and over in my head during the day, and then lying awake listening to Jo's scream on repeat in my head by night. It just consumed me. Grief. Loss. Sadness. Guilt!

Danny shifts in his seat, he wipes the tears with his hand.

Danny: It's been almost a year now, almost a year since she died. The police caught the bloke that did it. He told them I'd been coming onto him by looking at him funny in the club. He told them he didn't like the 'queer, bent bastard' giving him the come on. He told them he'd wanted to cut my throat to teach me a lesson. That the girl got in the way, that she was protecting the queer. It should have been me. I should have been lying in that ambulance, on that hospital bed, in the ground. Me. It should have been me. He should have killed me.

Danny pauses.

Danny: When they told me that, the police, when they told me what he'd said it just took hold inside me. The seed was already there; that seed of guilt, but once they told me what he said it grew and it consumed me. Consumed my thoughts. Filled my head. Jo's scream. My guilt. It just took over. It was like I was losing myself, who I was, to the grief. And the guilt.

Danny stands up, takes a few paces and then turns to face us.

Danny: At first I didn't sleep, so I tried sleeping tablets. Then I couldn't focus on work, so I tried anti-depressants. Then I couldn't go out and get pissed without fucking panic attacks on Old

Compton Street, so I started using whatever I could find to keep me high and take away the pain inside me. Sometimes I'd be wrecked for days but the drugs I took numbed the way I was feeling, and you can't feel guilt or grief when you're out of your head on whatever you can get your hands on.

Danny runs his hands through his hair, clasps his hands behind his head and takes a deep breath. He sits down again.

Danny: It was a few days before Christmas, I'd done some lines of coke, downed a shot... or several, drank what was left of the vodka I'd bought for Jo for Christmas and I decided to hit Soho and get wasted in the hope I'd be out of it until New Year. I thought some guy might take me back to his and I might not remember much until Big Ben had chimed in a great new year. Only that's not what happened. That's not the way it turned out.

Danny pauses.

Danny: When I woke up, I wasn't at some guy's flat I was on a bed in the hospital. It wasn't Adonis looking down at me; it was Jo. I remember squinting with the lights, looking at her eyes. They were beautiful, but full of hurt.

Danny shifts again in his seat, looking awkward.

Danny: Jo told me they were waiting for the On-Call Psych to see me. She told me they would help me; they would get me support. I told her, I was only fucking drunk, and had passed out because I'd had too much and couldn't handle it.

Beat.

Danny: They were there again... those beautiful eyes, full of hurt. Eyes full of grief and loss and sadness. And pain. And pity.

Danny lifts his arms and looks pointedly at his wrists. He rolls up the sleeves to his elbow, revealing deep scars on both wrists.

Danny: I've been in this unit for a few weeks now. They're getting me sorted. Off the drink. Off the drugs. Getting myself clean. The scream in my head has stopped too; my therapist said I'm coming to terms with the grief, and the loss and the guilt. She told me I'm making progress, that I can go home soon, as long as I am no longer a danger to myself or others.

Danny looks up and smiles, a half smile.

Danny: Jo visits every week, she told me she'd kill me if I tried to kill myself again. I'm not sure she realised what she'd said. She just took my hand and told me I'd never be on my own again, that together we would keep Sarah alive through our shared memories. Then she hugged me and told me everything was going to be alright. It felt good. I felt loved. Her hug felt like it went on for eternity.

Lights fade.

After the Silence - Part V: *Sarah*

"Angel" by Sarah McLachlan is playing.

Lights come up.

ENTER Sarah. Sarah is in her late 20s. Blond, beautiful, an English Rose. She is wearing an NHS gown and a dressing gown with pockets. Her make up is very understated. Sarah is dead.

She walks onto an empty stage.

The music fades out after the first chorus.

Sarah: It was this song. As I lay in the ambulance on the way to the hospital, this song came into my head. I remember my eyes closing and feeling a sudden calmness come over me. The pain I was in was easing. The tightness in my chest was relaxing. Everything just felt so calm. Still. Tranquil. I was at rest. I was at peace.

Beat.

Sarah: Of course it hadn't started out that way, that big night out with Danny. Big nights out with Danny were far from peaceful or tranquil – shots, cocktails, Steps, clubbing, dancing, drinking, more Steps, more shots. Being out with Danny was like being on some kind of rollercoaster, except you couldn't get off it until you'd thrown up in a doorway and had a McDonald's on the tube home.

Sarah is thoughtful.

Sarah: I think that's my biggest regret that night; Oh, no, not the McDonald's on the tube home; No. My biggest regret was that Danny didn't get to do his full routine to "Scared of the Dark" before, well before I was stabbed. I can't imagine how he must've felt, I mean it was our song, our anthem; I wonder if he still plays it and thinks of me.

Beat.

Sarah: I wonder if it was Danny who told mum about what had happened; I do hope she wasn't too upset; I'd lived life to the full with Danny Hutchinson. *Sarah smiles.* We had some wild times when we were kids. Playing out on the rec', pissing off Old Mrs Lucas next door with our pop concerts and fashion shows. I always thought I'd marry Danny one day... until he came out to me and told me he thought he was in love with H from Steps. I laughed at him and told him I fancied Lee, so it was fine and we could have a double wedding, only to realise a couple of years later that it was Claire I wanted, and so marriage and kids with Danny was well and truly scuppered with us **both** being gay.

Sarah becomes more serious.

Sarah: I remember the night I told mum. I'd been out with some of the girls... and Danny, to some quiz at the local pub. There was a waitress who I fancied, and Danny gave her my number and told me to ask her out. I did, and she told me her boyfriend was the one with the microphone, reading the questions. I was so embarrassed; totally mortified but of course Danny thought it was hilarious.

Beat.

Sarah: It was as we were walking home that it occurred to me; I couldn't tell my mum any of this without changing the story to (*grand voice*) 'The Waiter and the Girl with the Mircrophone'. I knew at that point I had to be honest and tell mum that I was a girl, who was into girls.

Sarah pauses.

Sarah: I don't know if it was shock, or disappointment, on her face. Shock at me being a lesbian, disappointment at not being the perfect daughter she'd bragged about. There was also a hint of rejection; more than a hint, a definite edge of rejection. My family, all I'd known since I was born, were rejecting me... because I wanted a Princess Charming, instead of a handsome Prince.

A pause.

Sarah: I heard her crying with dad for what seemed like hours. Next morning dad said nothing, just read his paper and asked me if I could pass him the milk for his tea, but mum wouldn't look me in the eye, she wouldn't acknowledge me - her own daughter. It was like I was no longer part of her.

Sarah smiles.

Sarah: She accepted me in time. Jo helped with that. I think when she saw I'd met somebody who made me happy, really happy, happy like her and dad (without the bickering), well with the bickering but with much better make-up sex - I hope! I think that's when she knew that I would be alright; that I wouldn't be a sad old lesbian spinster on my own with seven cats and KD Lang on repeat.

Sarah smiles to herself.

Sarah: Jo and I would be at mum and dad's every other Sunday. Mum would do a roast, I would take some flowers that I'd bought on the way and Jo would take a pudding. I think that's really what won mum over - the fact she had gained a daughter in law who baked like Mary Berry but with the sex appeal of Nigella! Jo's summer berry pavlova was the talk of mum's WI meetings – I swear she just wanted to get photographed naked behind Jo's stiff peaks of luscious meringue, like some kind of *Calendar Girl*.

Sarah sighs and takes a breath.

Sarah: It's the Sunday roasts I'll miss the most about mum and dad; Sunday visits generally to be honest. And the drive home with Jo, a piece of pavlova in an old Tupperware resting on my knee as Jo and I braved the journey back into London.

Beat.

Sarah: And Jo. Fuckin' hell I miss Jo. She was the love of my life, my soulmate, my forever girl. We were the perfect couple; she even accepted my GBF Danny! I hope she can move on, find another girl, someone to make her happy again... she deserves that.

Sarah pauses, becomes more serious.

Sarah: I just wish she'd been out that night so I could have told her I loved her. Given her a hug. Bought her a drink... and shown her this. *Sarah reaches into the dressing gown pocket and pulls out a positive pregnancy test.* I wish I could have told her that we were going to be parents – all three of us! Me, Jo and Danny.

Lights blackout.

Printed in Great Britain
by Amazon

59242421R00031